SQUEAKY SHOES

Written by Morgan Matthews
Illustrated by G. Brian Karas

Troll Associates

Library of Congress Cataloging in Publication Data

Matthews, Morgan.
Squeaky shoes.

Summary: When a shoemaking elf discovers no one will buy his shoes because they squeak, he decides to make quiet shoes called sneakers.

[1. Sneakers—Fiction. 2. Shoes—Fiction. 3. Fairies—Fiction] I. Karas, G. Brian, ill. II. Title.
PZ7.M43425Sq 1986 [E] 85-14014
ISBN 0-8167-0642-5 (lib. bdg.)
ISBN 0-8167-0643-3 (pbk.)

Printed in the United States of America

10 9 8 7 6 5 4 3 2 1

SQUEAKY SHOES

"Shoes for sale," called Elmo. "New shoes for sale! Buy my shoes!"

Elmo had a lot of shoes to sell. Elmo was an elf. Elmo Elf was a shoemaker.

Did you know that elves are the best shoemakers? They make very good shoes. And Elmo was the best shoemaker of all.

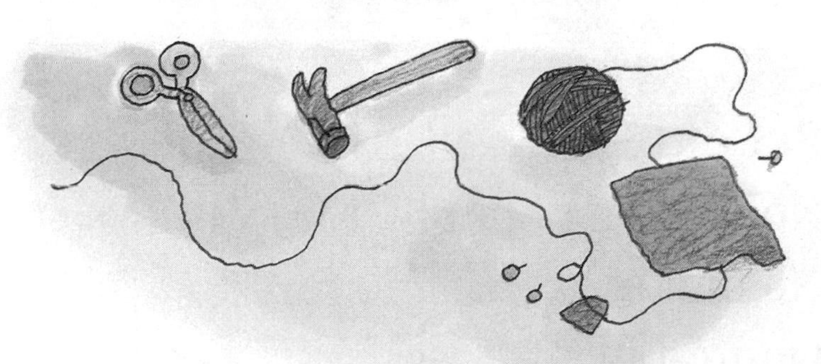

But did Elmo sell a lot of shoes?
No! No one bought Elmo's shoes.
No one in the magic forest
wanted new shoes.

Why? New shoes are squeaky. They squeak when you walk. They squeak and squeak! No one wanted squeaky shoes—and this is why!

In the magic forest lived a giant. He was very bad. He chased everyone he could find.
How did everyone get by the giant? Quietly, on tiptoes—they sneaked past the giant.

The wizard sneaked by the bad giant. When the fairy queen walked in the magic forest, she sneaked, too. Even the good witch sneaked by the giant. To sneak you must be quiet. And squeaky, new shoes are not quiet!

Elmo did not know about the giant. He did not know why his shoes did not sell. Poor Elmo Elf!
"No one wants my shoes," said Elmo. "I will not make shoes anymore. I will find a new job."

Elmo wanted to look his best. To find a job you must look good. He put on new shoes. Elmo put on squeaky, new shoes.

SQUEAK! SQUEAK! SQUEAK!
Away went Elmo to find a new job. Away he went in his squeaky, new shoes.

Elmo went to the wizard.
"I need a job," said Elmo. "Will
you give me a job?"
The wizard looked at Elmo.
"Can you dust?" said the wizard.
"My cave is dusty. I need
someone to dust my cave."

Elmo looked at the wizard's
cave.
"I know how to dust," said
Elmo. "I am a good duster. I
will dust your cave."

"Good," said the wizard. "You can have the job."

SQUEAK! SQUEAK! SQUEAK!
Elmo went into the dusty cave.
He dusted this. He dusted that.
Dust! Dust! Dust! Squeak!
Squeak! Squeak!

Elmo saw a dusty wand. It was the wizard's magic wand. Elmo dusted the magic wand. Suddenly—ZAP! Something happened. Elmo became a mouse. Poor Elmo Elf!

In came the wizard. He saw the wand. He saw the mouse. The wizard did not see Elmo.
"What happened?" asked the wizard.

The mouse squeaked. It squeaked and squeaked. "Quiet," said the wizard. "I know you are an elf and not a mouse. But be quiet! My pet dragon does not like mice. He chases mice."

The wizard used his magic. ZAP!
The mouse became Elmo.
"Go feed the dragon," said the
wizard. "And do not dust any
more wands."

Elmo went to feed the wizard's dragon. Squeak, squeak went his new shoes. Squeak! Squeak! Squeak!

Out came the dragon.
"No! No!" yelled Elmo. "I am not a mouse!"
But that squeaky noise sounded like a mouse to the dragon!

The dragon chased Elmo. It chased Elmo out of the cave. SQUEAK! SQUEAK! SQUEAK! Poor Elmo Elf!

“I do not want this job,” yelled Elmo. “This is not a good job. I do not like dusting magic wands. I do not like feeding pet dragons. I will find a new job.”

Away went Elmo. Squeak! Squeak! Squeak! Off he went to find a new job.

Elmo went to the good witch.
"Will you give me a job?" said Elmo.
"What can you do?" said the witch.
"I can dust," said Elmo. "Does your cave need dusting?"

The witch said, "No. My magic broom does the dusting. Can you stir witch's brew? My magic brew needs stirring."

"I know how to stir brew," said Elmo. "I am good at stirring witch's brew."
The witch looked at Elmo.
"The job is yours," she said.

Squeak! Squeak! Squeak! In went Elmo. He did not know witch's brew smells bad. Poor Elmo Elf!

Elmo stirred the smelly brew. "What a smell!" he yelled. "This brew smells bad. I do not like stirring smelly brew."

But stir he did. When he stirred his new shoes squeaked. He stirred and squeaked. He squeaked and stirred.

The witch's magic broom was dusting the cave. The broom liked quiet. It did not like squeaky, new shoes. What happened? The broom went after Elmo.

Tap!
"Ouch!" yelled Elmo. "Go away broom."
Tap! Tap! Tap!
"Ouch! Ouch! Ouch!"
The magic broom chased Elmo around the cave.

SQUEAK! SQUEAK! SQUEAK!
Tap! Tap! Tap!
"Ouch! Ouch! Ouch!"
Out of the witch's cave went
Elmo.

“I do not want this job,” yelled Elmo. “I do not like stirring smelly brew. I do not like magic brooms. I will get a job with the fairy queen.”

The fairy queen lived in the magic forest. Into the magic forest went Elmo. Squeak! Squeak! Squeak!

Elmo did not know about the bad giant. He did not know he should sneak quietly by. He was not quiet. Elmo did not sneak. He squeaked!

"Squeaking!" yelled the giant.
"Who is squeaking in my forest?"
Out came the giant. He saw
Elmo Elf.
"I'll get you!" he called.

The giant chased Elmo. Away went the elf. SQUEAK! SQUEAK! SQUEAK! The giant chased Elmo out of the forest.

"A giant in the forest," said Elmo. "Squeaky shoes made him find me. So that is why no one wants to buy my new shoes. I will make quiet shoes."

Elves are good shoemakers. Elmo Elf was the best shoemaker of all. His new shoes did not squeak. They were quiet and good for sneaking.
"I will call my new shoes *sneakers*," said Elmo.

Elmo put on sneakers. Out he
went to sell his new shoes.
"Sneakers for sale," called Elmo.
"Quiet shoes for sneaking by the
giant. Buy my sneakers."

Everyone liked Elmo's quiet, new shoes. Everyone wanted sneakers. The fairy queen bought sneakers.

The good witch bought sneakers.

The wizard bought sneakers. Elmo sold lots and lots of sneakers. He even sold sneakers to the wizard's pet dragon.

They all loved their new sneakers. Except, of course, for the giant, who wondered why the magic forest had become such a quiet place!